THE MERCY THAT ENDURETH

Oluwafemi O. Emmanuel

Published by Revival Waves of Glory Books & Publishing

PO Box 596 | Litchfield, Illinois 62056 USA

www.revivalwavesofgloryministries.com

Revival Waves of Glory Books & Publishing is committed to excellence in the publishing industry.

Published in the United States of America

Paperback: 978-1-387-05758-0

Table of Contents

CHAPTER 1:
INTRODUCTION

THE MERCIFUL GOD

Psalm 136:6

"Oh give thanks unto the LORD; for He is good: for His mercies endureth forever"

I will be discussing about three points which this reference of the Bible above is revealing unto us.

- **Giving thanks unto the LORD**

Giving thanks to Jehovah Lord our God the Almighty is worth doing. Many people usually give thanks mainly for what God has done already, but have we made it an attitude to give Him thanks because of what He is capable of doing, and because of who He is?

Our God is an awesome God, who reigns on high; the God of Heaven and the earth. He is powerful, glorious, and excellent in all His ways, He has never lost any battle and will never lose any battle, His dominion is from eternity past before the world began, He still reigns now when the world is, and would still continue to reign through eternity. Nevertheless, He is also dangerous and terrible in His ways; that is, His vengeance cannot be waited for and should be avoided, and He is a marvelous God. No one could really describe how great He is. But yet He still rules in the affairs of His creations; ready to have a cordial relationship with us, even though we are unstable in our ways, yet He still choose to commune with us. Wow, and that makes the Bible to introduce the next phrase.

- **For He is good**

The goodness of God cannot be compared to anything that may be termed "good" by man. Christ Himself was even telling the people with Him that no one in human flesh could conclude on what a perfect goodness is, that is, there will always be a setback in human capacity toward a perfect goodness. But in God only can a man be good (John 15:5). Then how according to the portion of the Bible is He good?

- **His Mercies endureth forever**

Mercy, this is God's nature; it is compassion, forbearance and forgiving, having pity, a grace beyond measure, a love, a care and a blessing.

As we have examined so little in the personality of God, how do you think He should relate with man.

Job 7:17

"What is man, that thou shouldest magnify him? and that thou shouldest set thine heart upon him? And that thou shouldest visit him every morning, and try him every moment?"

Does He have to grant him free will; that is man making choice for himself and indulging himself regardless of the will of his creator? Does He have to set His affections toward them by caring for them? Did He have to send Jesus Christ His only begotten Son that He might die for him? Does He have to reveal His mind unto him? And does He have to give him thousands of chances and wait for him to repent?

Now, if man is supposed to possess the personality of God how will he relates with other living things inferior to him; will he endure their trespasses and transgressions, will he make them make choices as they wish and still be patience for them to repent from their evil ways? Will he endure any foul and unbelief pronouncement on him by his inferiors? Indeed, God is so good to us and His mercies endureth forever.

However since in the beginning according to Genesis 6:6 the Bible makes us to understand that man had reached the peak of his wickedness to the extent that God repented that He had created man and that should be thousands of years ago, still up to this moment the mercy of God wax stronger; He is capable to forgive man million times a day. And so as wicked man is, yet the mercy of the Lord never weakens, the degree of sin never rendered It impotent, and the transgression of man never reduces Its strength. Once a man repents, every of his trespass shall be forgiven and forgotten because the patient of mercy never get wearied out; it became renewed every morning and so it endures forever.

Grace and Mercy.

Today, many Christians don't know the difference between Grace and Mercy. Even though my discussion is on mercy, but to know the relationship between the two we will have to go a little into grace in comparison to mercy.

It is made known that grace is basically getting what you don't deserve, of which what is best been used as an example is salvation; giving us the power and privilege to become a child of God, and to draw nearer unto Him not again by sacrifice but simply by the faith in the Son of God –Jesus, who died for our sins. And this also is the strength beyond our normal capacity, a strong positive temperament, a talent, and simply a free gift of nature from the Most-High God, the Creator of the heaven and earth. At the other hand, Mercy is said to be not getting or escaping what one deserved: like most especially judgement. An example is that of a lady's testimony some years ago, of how she survived from failing a particular course subject at school, according to her story when she saw the questions at first glance she thought she was already a failure because she didn't know the answers to the questions at all, eventually she wrote something as to show an attempt towards the question even though she wrote wrong answers, and to the examiner after the submission of the papers it was a total rubbish and in furiousness the examiner made two question mark on her paper as a sign of a total incorrect answers. But when it got to the person who would record the scores the person though the was seeing 77 instead of two question marks (??), and fortunately for her, the person who was recording the final score wrote 77 without examining the content, and that was how she pass through the exam. On a normal day she deserved to be failed but she was favoured. Mercy; she didn't get what she deserved. In the book of Jonah, the Bible makes us to understand that the people of Nineveh deserved to be destroy, but instead God sent Jonah to them that they may repent so as to withdraw the judgement prepared for them, and in chapter 3:10 when God saw that they repented He turned away His judgement and in chapter 4:11 God concluded that they were ignorant, even though Nineveh was one of the enemies of His people–Israel in those days and every enemies of the people of God are also enemies to God, but yet God chose to have mercy on them.

But mercy is actually more than escaping judgment one deserves. In other words Where strength could not prevail again, in total confusion and a hopeless state where all what you have tried has failed and no one is there to help, and sometimes not that they don't want to but they actually don't know how to because it is beyond their understanding, and you dropped everything to let go, then miracle happens. This is when you don't understand how you manage to succeed exceedingly in your little endeavor as it may seem to you, or when you are the only one who is accepted among others irrespective of other's personality that may serve as an advantage to them to be preferred over you. While Grace is a gift from God, Mercy stands to be the nature of God; showing compassion on those who He will show compassion; irrespective of size or level, pasts, personality, aptitude, attitude, ability and or capability.

Grace is much active while we are still in this world; when we are not yet dead. But mercy goes as far as standing to plead before the judgement throne of God after we are dead that we might be brought back to life that we might make amend or restitute where necessary (this do happen sometimes when the miracle of bringing the dead to life is been done by God through His servants). That is, where one rejects the grace of salvation through Christ Jesus over and over again and died and then deserves to be condemned and yet God still brings him back to life that he might have yet another chance to forsake his ways, then he is said to have obtained mercy. When we fall from grace we get judgement, but when mercy intervenes then judgement will be abolished.

Grace can metamorphose or grow to become mercy. When grace is been said to be extravagant or exceeding or great especially in the case of forgiveness of sins then it can appear to be the work of mercy (as given in Eph. 1:6; 2:4-6 talking about rich grace and glorious grace). That is why sometimes what we hear or experienced that we see as grace could correlates with the work of mercy and by that we thought they are the same. But however, they do work together as simple as when you don't get what you deserved (mercy) which is the severe punishment fits for your sin, then you will actually get what you don't deserve (grace) –a salvation and a pardon. When there is activation of mercy then grace flows in like a river.

And yet in summary of some differences between the two goes thus:

By grace we received salvation, by mercy we escape judgments.

By grace we exceed in our endeavors, by mercy we exceeds miraculously even at the point where failure seems to be inevitable.

By grace we withstand the temptations without falling, by mercy we are pardoned even if we fall into temptation.

By grace we are given and make proper use of our talents and gifts for excellence, but by mercy we excel even without showcasing much of our talents.

Grace expires; it has a time limit (the Bible doesn't say "Grace endureth forever" but even says in Romans 6 that grace has limitations), but mercy endures; it also makes extension of time.

Grace makes us pray fervently without getting wearied, but only by mercy will God answer our prayers.

While grace gives an exceeding (explainable) enablement for a breakthrough, mercy makes happens a miracle (an unexplainable occurrence) for a breakthrough.

CHAPTER 2:
HIS MERCY OVER THE CREATION

His mercy as a love over His creation

Psalm 145:9

"The Lord is good to all: and His tender mercies are over all His works"

After God created the universe He immediately fell in love with it; He looked upon it and thought it was pleasant and good in His eyes. In this world today as we have it, there are many creatures and not all of it is adorable, in fact I'd say 40% is not. There are creature we cannot associate ourselves with not even move close to them or try and kill for food; some because they are dangerous, some because they have a fierce appearance most especially creepy animals, even though some are harmless but because you will feel nausea and or uncomfortable already by looking at them you will tend to flee from it or kill it because they are not pleasant to the eyes, some like insects and rodent seems to be troublesome, some appearance are too disturbing to see, many of it are in the water, and the snake which seems to be that one of God's curses for it (Gen 3:15,16) made it one of the most hated creature to man. But yet all these creatures are good and pleasant before God.

When God would flood the earth, he made all animals to march two by two into the ark that they might not be a victim of destruction and annihilation. And there after forty days of heavy raining, the Bible says "And God remembered Noah and every Living Creature" in that ark. That is, He didn't let alone Noah to be remembered but also every living animals equally has He had remembered Noah and his family—really it's wonderful. He took compassion on every living animal that they may not get involved in the sharing of His wrath and that they may continue in their existence and not going extinct.

The instinct impact for survival

God gave man wisdom to execute his plans whatsoever it may be to sustain him. But God gave animals instinct to carry out its survival plans; no wisdom, no knowledge neither understanding, yet they survive but what made them seems to be intelligent in their operations is their instinct. This is not by chance as evolution proves, but it is divinely engineered by the great and merciful God. The animals would have been impotent and dunce to the extreme if not for this power of instinct, and there survival rates would have been very low. But God in His compassion over His creation made Him to create this instinct in them to make them survive, from the greatest to the smallest creatures. This instinct drives them to do the right thing at the right time and at any given environment; most especially to make shelter for them and to take a good care for their babies.

God's mercy as acre over his creation

Matthew 6:26, 29-30

"Behold the fowls of the air: for they sow not, neither do they reap, nor gather into barns; yet your heavenly father feedeth them….And why ye take thought for raiment? Consider the lilies of the field, how they grow; they toil not, neither do they spin: and yet I say unto you, that even Solomon in all his glory was not arrayed like one of these. Wherefore, if God so clothe the grass of the field, which today is, and tomorrow is cast into the oven, shall he not much more clothe you, O ye of little faith?"

This passage above pastes a very good picture about the love of God over His creation; God design so well the non-living things in their specific glory; to beautify and make pleasantness out of nature; trees, flowers, rocks and mountains, ocean and sea, lakes and rivers all in their individual beauty, and the Bible says when God look at them all they are all good and satisfying to God.

Then also it shows that every animals despite the size and ability are fed by God.

Sparrow, as it is written in Matthew 10:29 that two of it is sold for just a penny to show how little in worth as equivalent to its size. But the Bible makes us to understand that yet God cares about it so much that He is highly interested in its wellbeing. Not because it is a small or a vulnerable creature, but it is because it is actually one of God's creation. God, as He cares for the little Sparrow so also He cares for all His creation whether great or small, land animal or sea animal, irrespective of the degree of the intelligence.

An Ostrich as the Bible has described it, so it is in its real nature. The Bible made us to understand that it has a very low intelligent compare to other animals, unlike other animals: it lacks good parenthood instinct; after it lay it eggs it leaves it on the bare ground and thus makes it susceptible to be preyed on, and yet they are yet to go extinct.

A Kiwi lays only one egg, it barely see and cannot fly, it leaves in a hole on under the ground, not that fast and as small as a domestic chicken, yet they still live up to this moment without being in extinction.

An elephant gives birth to only one baby unlike other animals, yet they are yet to go extinct.

The Bible also talks about horses as highly as they are used in wars then, yet they are not extinct till date. All this are the result of God's mercy in care.

Some animals sleep as long as 14 hours a day, and yet they are still fed, some animals are very slow in nature and yet they never lack. Some animals that are strong in the kingdom sometimes lacks more than some animals that seems weak. Some animals are so vulnerable to the extent that they spent half of their lives running from predators and yet they live long. Food chain as it is, it has been happening over thousands of years, yet many has never through it gone into extinction. Before domestic animals are domesticated, as small and vulnerable as they are in the midst of their predators, they are still yet to go extinct. This is God's care over His creation.

Some animals live where water is scarce yet they don't go dehydrated or die of thirst, the Lord make them to survive on the little they get. Some animals could live a long time without food and yet survive, some sleep for 2 years and not die. As scientist discover some extinct animals so also they are discovering new species of animal every day and there are yet some animals that are yet to be discovered.

He made Himself the overseer of all

After the fallen of man the nature has gone out of control of man. The only administration of man to the other creature as divinely ordained is the (Adam's) 'christening' and thereafter is (Noah's) 'salvaging', but thereafter man got himself relieved by sin from the administration of animal overseeing, all what man is doing is just rearing of animals for food or as pet. Most of damages and hazard in the world today are basically from man, and by science they kept on toiling with the stability of nature. Many-a-times plants and animals contribute to the survivor and wellbeing of its world; they are sometimes a great supervisor to their every own flora and fauna. But as a matter of facts, man with his fierce and selfish intelligent is destroying his planet. But the mercy of God sustained the wellbeing of the earth and its inhabitant and no degree of man's violent act has been able to utterly destroy the earth because it is of the LORD and the fullness thereof.

He own us

Matthew 5:45

"…That ye may be the children of your father which is in heaven: for he maketh His sun to rise on the evil and unto good, and sendeth rain on the just and the unjust"

This passage established the fact that everyone on the planet earth is owned and cared for by God, believer or not believer. And as a matter of truth everyone is owned by God in two ways:

By Creation (Genesis 2:7): The Bible makes us to understand that man was given a breath even from the Almighty God Himself, which means man which was formed from the earth was given a life (intelligence, will, emotion and all that entails in the personality of man that makes him different from the animals) by God's breath and by that every identity of man is being given by God; He knows everyone by name, and so He has decided to keep His responsibility intact for every human being on earth irrespective of their imperfect lives.

By Redemption (Romans 3:23-25): The Bible made clear that everyone is a sinner and sin makes us an enemy of God; it makes one to be unfit and deserving a severe penalty, and thus we are being made a slave unto the prince of the world which is Satan to control our affairs, and that is why today we are experiencing the achievement of evil much more than good achievement in our world. And every efforts of man to be righteous prove abortive as the Bible says "…as filthy rags". But the redemption of man came through Christ Jesus by His death that we might have a forgiveness of sin, a perfect righteous life and be a partaker of God's inheritance (Heb. 9:15). And so therefore those who God owned by redemption greater inheritance that will last forever will be their portion

Either by creation or by redemption, it is a nice thing to hear that God still cares about man, for He said "…leave them, let them grow together" that is He is still watching over the children of men to nourishing them together both the good and the bad with the free gifts of nature; the air to breath, the water to drink, food from the plants and animals and all these are the works of God which man still benefits from and despite the rebellion of man God never stops the growth and the reproduction of plants and animals yielding in their particular season that they might serve as food. And so also Man should think about his sleeps and his waking up that it is not by his might; when he sleeps who guilds the holes of his nose and ears that dangerous insect may not enter, sleep is like a death this is when the brain and the nerves of the body is being put to rest you could never decide for the brain to start working or not and that is if to wake up or not, this also is when the body is very much susceptible to any sort of harm but yet we still sleep and wake up and think it is normal. But by God's mercy millions of people's faith in waking up after a long sleep is been honoured. So if God could show a great care towards man irrespective of his unbelief in Him how much greater care will He show if he believe and be redeemed.

The children and our everyday activities

When God says children are His heritage, He definitely proves it by the degree of His protection over them. There are activities of children that are dangerous to them, they can eat anything they see, and they can play with toxin objects or agents unknowing to them, their parents or guardians and so on like that, and yet most of them are always healthy. And so I tell you that you can never take care of your children as God would. If God does not build the house they labour in vain that builds it.

Doctor's reports these days shows that most of our habits in our daily living that we see as normal are actually dangerous to our health, for example they reveal that many of our fast food delicacies are actually junk foods and that there are many food, water and beverage poisoning, and also the normal posture of our sitting when in the toilet is actually wrong and they told us that squirting is the best posture, they told us that sitting for hours doing anything whatsoever is actually wrong, most of our posture when sleeping and the way we rise from bed is wrong, and almost all our everyday activities are done wrongly pertaining with the issue of health sometimes they call it dangerous or bad habit, industrial waste causing air pollution and water pollution. They say some of these usually results to cancer, and we are given some instructions to observe that we might live healthy. But in spite of all these report, we are still living healthy. What I'm really saying here is that the Mercy of God disregards the principle for healthy living when in operations. We seems to have many doctors and principles of healthy livings in this generation more than those olden days, and yet people lived long in those days, babies and their mothers survived without anti-natal and post-natal as effective and advance as it is today, no frequent reports of sickle-cell syndrome, cancer, HIV and AIDS, and other related diseases, and it seems that those local medicines in those days are very effective. All these happened because God made himself the overseer of His creation even to the unlearned generations.

CHAPTER 3:
GOD'S MERCY AS A COMPASSION AND FORGIVENESS OVER SINNERS

Now after we have seen little in the previous chapter how God is so merciful to the world in general either good people or bad people, I will like us to see God's compassion for the souls of men in the forgiveness and redemption of man individually. God extended the arms of mercy upon the children of men by seeing it pleasurable to call everyone His children, the Bible makes us to understand that it is a great expression of love of God toward us (1 John 3). That is why He sent His son Jesus to die for us that we might receive the forgiveness of sin, the adoption of God, and the eternal inheritance of His Kingdom.

Jesus the compassionate

When Jesus came into the world, throughout His earthly life was an encapsulation of the demonstration of mercy; He demonstrated the best love ever by giving Himself for us. He healed the sick, raised the dead, and everyone that cried upon Him both Israelites and the gentiles were all attended to. Some of the people Jesus attended to moved Jesus with their faith (even the gentiles, which are the centurion in Matt 8, and the Canaanite woman in Matt 15 and so on), of which means that even today Jesus still attend to the unbelievers but that is when they call upon Him at their worst situation and when they apply faith as little as it may be.

Jesus approached some to be healed like the impotent man at the pool in John 5, disregarding his complaint, and that is what compassion does; it disregards the unbelief and double-mind of the person that it engages with. And that is why you see even the skeptics receiving their miracles in an evangelical gathering.

He demonstrated the compassion of the highest other by miraculously feeding the five thousand (diverse kind of) people: those that believed and those that didn't believe in Him, sinners and the righteous and so on. Which means His compassion is not limited by the quantity of the people; it can work for people collectively, for example He can have compassion upon the whole congregation of the church, and also upon the whole family members either nuclear or extended, and also upon the nation.

He averted the judgement of sin over the sinners.

There are four types of different cases of mercy as forgiveness over sinners by Jesus Christ in the New Testament that I will want to use as a case study:

1. Luke 7:36-39; She Went to Jesus with her "big" sin.

"And, behold, a woman in the city, <u>which was a sinner,</u> when she knew that Jesus sat at the meat in the Pharisee's house, brought an alabaster box of ointment, and stood at his feet behind him weeping, and began to wash his feet with tears, and did wipe them with the hairs of her head, and kissed his feet, and anointed them with the ointment.

Now when the Pharisee which had bidden him saw it and spake within himself, saying, This man, if he were a prophet, would have known <u>who and what manner of woman this is</u> that toucheth him: for she is a sinner"

This unnamed woman above was made obvious of who she was by how the author of this book of Luke has presented her "A woman in city, which was a sinner" that is, everyone in the city knew her as a sinner, probably an harlot (as they usually was as a woman then), or a necromancer etc. but the type of a title they could give her is "a sinner" which means she must be a well-known by her status. Another thing is according to the thought of the Pharisees when they said "…who and what manner of woman this is" that is, they tried to express the type of sinner she was and the degree of her sins.

But Jesus, to show them that He knew quite well the degree of her sins. He told the story of two debtors: one with five hundred pence and other fifty. Now to compare the woman with the one owning five hundred pence (according to how Jesus had related the story with the case of the woman in His conversation He made with Simon) shows that Jesus knew how great her sins was. But when she went to Jesus and wept as she felt sorry for her sins, immediately she was forgiven.

2. John 8:7-8; She was Brought Forth for Judgement

"So when they continued asking Him, He lifted up Himself, and said unto them, He that is without sin among you, let him first cast a stone at her. And again He stooped down, and wrote on the ground. And they which heard it, being convicted by their own conscience, went out one by one, beginning at the eldest, even unto the last: and Jesus was left alone, and the woman standing in the midst.

When Jesus had lifted up Himself, and saw none but the woman, He said unto her, Woman, where are those thine accusers? Hath no man condemned thee? She said No man,

Lord. And Jesus said unto her <u>neither do I condemn thee</u>, go, and sin no more."

This also an unnamed woman unlike the first one was condemned; it may be that that was her first, or she may also be a harlot, condition may have pushed her to the situation, or it may be a set-up for the lady to get Jesus to misjudge her. But whichever way, she was condemned and people were aroused and was ready to get her stoned. And so also unlike the first woman she didn't come to Jesus willingly but was pushed to Jesus for a judgement. But getting to Jesus, reverse was the case; instead of getting judgement, she got mercy, instead of getting condemnation she was discharged and acquitted. Hallelujah.

3. Mark 2:3-5; He Didn't Realize that he Needed Forgiveness of Sin

"And they come unto Him bringing one sick of the palsy which was borne on four. And when they could not come nigh unto Him for the press, they uncovered the roof where He was: and when they had broken it up, they let down the bed wherein the sick of the palsy laid. When Jesus saw their faith, He said unto the sick of the palsy, Son, thy sin be forgiven thee."

In the case of this man, unlike the two women above, no one actually knew he was a sinner who may have gotten himself on the sick bed by his sins. Apparently he didn't come for forgiveness but actually came for healing, but irrespective of the fact that he has not come with a genuine and convicted heart for a pardon and it didn't even occur to him that he needed it to be perfectly healed. Yet Jesus saw the need for him to be forgiven; actually to give him a perfect healing, and so at that moment he was forgiven and healed. Such case still happens today.

4. Mark 5-19; Jesus Sought for him that he might be Forgiven

"Howbeit Jesus suffered him not, but saith unto him, Go home to thy friends, and tell them how great things the Lord hath done for thee, and hath had <u>compassion on thee"</u>

This is Jesus talking here to the man of Gadara. This short story with this man of Gadara seems to have many hidden details. The details we can perceive from the actions of the Gadarenes, the details we can perceive from the word of Christ to him, the details we can perceive from his dwelling place, the details we can perceive from the nature of his sickness, the details we can perceive from the dialogue of Jesus and the demons, and the details we can perceive from the relationship of Jesus and the town. These details were not given as a record but we should surely know that there are big events undisclosed on this matter that would or may have happened, before and after Jesus visited this town only once in His earthly life. But one thing calls for a good notice which is when Jesus told him to go home and tell about the compassion of God on him. And talking of compassion then we cannot overrule sin.

The statement of Jesus to this man shows that he was redeemed from sin and healed from his afflictions. Jesus only went to the town just because of him, it's just like saying Jesus did not really pay the whole town a visit but only visited this mad man, bond physically and spiritually to be forgiven from his sins.

It is good that one should be convicted of his sins after hearing the Gospel and asked for forgiveness, but do you know that sometime when mercy found someone—a sinner, he won't be waited for to come and repent before God will reveal Himself to him, many are visited by God Himself like Saul of Tarsus in Act 9, it may be through open vision, or in the dream. As we can see from those cases above that some people approach God for forgiveness and some are approached by God that they may be forgiven. In either ways, anyone who have accepted God's proposal of forgiveness are forgiven instantly.

Now here we have four kinds of sinners with different types of cases and different types of approach: one went to Jesus directly for forgiveness; one was pushed to Jesus for judgement; it didn't occur to one that he needed forgiveness; one was even out of himself –from his conscious mind, he never had any idea that someone could come for him; people are aware that some from these people are sinners; one was not seen as a sinner but only a sick person, some were rejected while one was assisted, one asked for forgiveness, while others didn't ask. But they were all met and forgiven, "Not of him that willeth or of him that runneth, but it's of the Lord that showeth mercy".

Jesus Christ the great compassionate; concerning Him the Bible makes these beautiful and powerful statements:

- Isaiah 9:6

    For unto us a Child is born, unto us a Son is given: and the government shall be upon his shoulder: and his name shall be called Wonderful, Counsellor, The mighty God, The everlasting Father, The Prince of Peace. 7 Of the increase of His government and peace there shall be no end, upon the throne of David, and upon his kingdom, to order it, and to establish it with judgment and with justice from henceforth even forever. The zeal of the Lord of hosts will perform this.

- John 1:1-14

In the beginning was the Word, and the Word was with God, and the Word was God. ² The same was in the beginning with God. ³ All things were made by Him; and without him was not anything made that was made. ⁴ In him was life; and the life was the light of men. ⁵ And the light shineth in darkness; and the darkness comprehended it not... ⁹That was the true Light, which lighteth every man that cometh into the world. ¹⁰ He was in the world, and the world was made by Him, and the world knew Him not. ¹¹ He came unto His own, and His own received him not. ¹² But as many as received Him, to them gave He power to become the sons of God, even to them that believe on His name: ¹³ Which were born, not of blood, nor of the will of the flesh, nor of the will of man, but of God. ¹⁴ And the Word was made flesh, and dwelt among us, (and we beheld his glory, the glory as of the only begotten of the Father,) full of grace and truth.

- Proverb 18:22-36

The Lord possessed Me in the beginning of His way, before His works of old. ²³ I was set up from everlasting, from the beginning, or ever the earth was. ²⁴ When there were no depths, I was brought forth; when there were no fountains abounding with water. ²⁵*Before the mountains were settled, before the hills was I brought forth:* ²⁶ *While as yet He had not made the earth, nor the fields, nor the highest part of the dust of the world.* ²⁷ *When He prepared the heavens, I was there: when He set a compass upon the face of the depth:* ²⁸ *When He established the clouds above: when He strengthened the fountains of the deep:* ²⁹ *When He gave to the sea his decree, that the waters should not pass His commandment: when He appointed the foundations of the earth:* ³⁰ *Then I was by Him, as one brought up with Him: and I was daily His delight, rejoicing always before Him;* ³¹ *Rejoicing in the habitable part of His earth; and My delights were with the sons of men.* ³² *Now therefore hearken unto Me, O ye children: for blessed are they that keep My ways.* ³³ *Hear instruction, and be wise, and refuse it not.* ³⁴ *Blessed is the man that heareth Me, watching daily at my gates, waiting at the posts of my doors.* ³⁵ *For whoso findeth Me findeth life, and shall obtain favour of the Lord.* ³⁶ *But he that sinneth against me wrongeth His own soul: all they that hate Me love death.*

- Hebrews 1:1

God, who at sundry times and in divers manners spake I time past unto the fathers by the prophets, Hath in these last days spoken unto us by His Son, whom He hath appointed heir of all things, by whom also He made the worlds; Who being the brightness of His glory, and the express image of His person, and upholding all things by the word of His power, when He had by Himself purged our sins, sat down on the right of the majesty on High…But unto His son He saith, Thy throne, O God, is forever and ever: a sceptre of righteousness of thy Kingdom.

- Philippians 2:6

  Who, although being essentially one with God and in the form of God [possessing the fullness of the attributes which make God God], did not think this equality with God was a thing to be eagerly grasp or retained (AMP)

- 2 Corinthians 5:21

  For He hath made Him[self] to be sin for us, who knew no sin; that we might be made a righteousness of God in Him.

- Isaiah 53:1-51

  Who hath believed our report? and to whom is the arm of the Lord revealed? [2]For He shall grow up before Him as a tender plant, and as a root out of a dry ground: He hath no form nor comeliness; and when we shall see Him, there is no beauty that we should desire Him. [3] He is despised and rejected of men; a man of sorrows, and acquainted with grief: and we hid as it were our faces from Him; He was despised, and we esteemed Him not. 4 Surely He hath borne our griefs, and carried our sorrows: yet we did esteem Him stricken, smitten of God, and afflicted. 5 But He was wounded for our transgressions, He was bruised for our iniquities: the chastisement of our peace was upon Him; and with His stripes we are healed. 6 All we like sheep have gone astray; we have turned every one to his own way; and the Lord hath laid on Him the iniquity of us all.7 He was oppressed, and He was afflicted, yet He opened not his mouth: He is brought as a lamb to the slaughter, and as a sheep before her shearers is dumb, so He openeth not his mouth. 8 He was taken from prison and from judgment: and who shall declare His generation? for He was cut off out of the land of the living: for the transgression of my people was He stricken. 9 And He made his grave with the wicked, and with the rich in his death; because he had done no violence, neither was any deceit in his mouth. 10 Yet it pleased the Lord to bruise Him; He hath put Him to grief: when thou shalt make his soul an offering for sin, He shall see his seed, He shall prolong His days, and the pleasure of the Lord shall prosper in his hand. 11 He shall see of the travail of His soul, and shall be satisfied: by His knowledge shall my righteous servant justify *many; for He shall bear their iniquities. ¹² Therefore will I divide Him a portion with the great, and He shall divide the spoil with the strong; because He hath poured out his soul unto death: and he was numbered with the transgressors; and He bare the sin of many, and made intercession for the transgressors.*

- 1 Timothy 3:16

And without controversy great is the mystery of godliness: God was manifest in the flesh, justified in the Spirit, seen of angels, preached unto the Gentiles, believed on in the world, received up into glory.

- Philippians 2:9

Wherefore God hath highly exalted Him, and given Him a name which is above every other name ¹⁰ That at the name of Jesus every knees should bow, of things in heaven, and things in earth, and things under the earth. ¹¹And that every tongue should confess that Jesus Christ is Lord, to the glory of the Father.

All these great and wonderful reports above in summary reveals the position of Christ as God, and yet it pleases Him to come to the world He created, walked on the surface of the earth is His, related with human which are the work of His hand; He talked with them, ate with them, argued with them and at the end He chose to surrender Himself to be crucified that every man might be saved. And that is the true definition and demonstration of an act of compassion (mercy).

The Mercy Seat (Exodus 25:26)

In the Old Testament when the LORD ask Moses to build Him a tent that He might dwell among them. Therein are furniture of different kind, but the one that represented the glory and the presence of God is the Ark of Covenant, and while others are place outside the tent (such as the brazen alter and the golden laver) and some inside the holy tent (such as the golden lamp-stand, the shew bread table and the golden alter), the Ark of Covenant only was placed inside the holy of holies. It is so sacred that it has to be visited once in a year and only by the priests. But upon it was the Mercy Seat and this Mercy Seat is been initiated by God purposely to show compassion because the content inside of the Covenant Ark is what could remind the Israelite of how unworthy they are, most especially the Ten Commandment on the Tablet inside of which is what the Israelite cannot obey perfectly and so the Mercy Seat is the favour they receive from God because even in their unworthiness and imperfection God still dwelled with them, and so whenever God sees the Mercy Seat then the unworthiness and imperfection of the congregation will be erased. The congregation of Israel could not withstand the presence of God represented by the Ark of Covenant, but the Mercy Seat makes them worthy to receive God's presence into their midst. And that is why it is called the Mercy Seat. This shows how compassionate God is to His people even though over many years the Israelites wander away from the presence of God yet He did not totally forsake them but rather create another means by which His people will be closer to Him.

The LORD Merciful and Gracious (Exodus 33:18-ch34:7)

God made it known unto Moses that nobody sees Him and lived, but when God saw the desire of Moses to see Him, He decided to reveal Himself by His presence. And to show Moses that what he was about to experience is what can be only done by the involvement of mercy; the God that created the universe, whose reign is from the eternity past and that is why He is called The Ancient of Days, and who will still reign in the eternity future and that is why He is called the everlasting God, revealing Himself in a very open vision to an ordinary man who is made a little lower than the angel, who whose righteousness is as filthy as rags, who drink iniquity like water, whose days is like that of a grass which blossom in the morning and withered in the evening, a man whose years if graced with strength would only live a hundred years without feebleness, a man which can never be perfect. But God said He will have mercy on who He will have mercy.

Exodus 34:6-7

"And the LORD passed by before him (Moses), and proclaimed, The LORD, The LORD God, merciful and gracious, longsuffering, and abundant in goodness and truth, keeping mercy for thousands, forgiving iniquity and transgression and sin, and that will by no means clear the guilty; visiting the iniquity of the fathers upon the children's children, unto the third and to the fourth generation"

This proclamation in the reference above is actually a panegyric which restrained the execution of the inevitable judgement for seeing God of which was proclaimed by Heaven Himself, which means that the mercy Moses obtained in seeing God and not being consumed was what was fully backed up by the whole Heaven. The panegyric emphasized the true nature of God, which means therefore that taking God by His word and eulogizing His true nature makes God to be moved to break protocol to do something in advantage of His people no matter how unworthy the situation may seems. God is still very much in the business of revealing

Himself to His children, He is not less concern about how people perish without obtaining mercy. So this is still a great news for everyone on earth; even though the kingdom of God may seems difficult but yet I tell you as you are reading this book, that God is still willing to save you no matter how unworthy it may seems you are as long as you surrender yourself to Him and be subjected in your humility to truth of His personality, and that's what the eulogy of "The LORD God Merciful and Gracious".

God's compassion over backsliders

2 Chronicle 7:14 says *"If my people who are called by my name, shall humble themselves, and pray, and seek my face and turn from their wicked ways; then will I hear from heaven, and will heal their land"*.

This passage is directly referring to those that had known God initially, but has later gone astray. God's compassion on His people who have compromised makes God not to give up on them, irrespective of the degree of the offence and how much it has being. Whenever I meditate about God's "plea" in Isaiah 1:18, I felt it to be a great result of a solemn love, this I called a mother of all loves, a charity that will never let go of her own under any circumstances: the love of the prodigal son's father and the love that initiated the death of Christ on the cross. I would never have imagine God calling softly and tenderly to the ordinary man that has already turned his back on Him for a dialogue or for a negotiation of which if it turns unfruitful will not affect God but only add to or aggravate the peril or woe of the man, and that sounds ridiculous to me against God, but yet God did not take it as ridicule but the expression of His love and compassion.

As I said earlier, mercy is a nature of God, which is why it is very easy for Him to forgive and forget our sins and avert every prophecies of judgement against sinners, that is why God said according to the book of Ezekiel 33:14-16, that if He say [aforetime] that a sinner will die, but if the sinner repents afterward and forsake his ways, then the death pronouncement will be averted and the sin will not be put to mind again. Then the Bible makes us to understand the compassion of God toward sinners and the sinful world, as we have gotten many instances in the Bible:

- 1 Peter 3:20 and Numbers 14:18 talks about the mercy of God as a long-suffering that sinners may repent and be saved before He comes with judgement.

- Jeremiah in Lamentation 3:22 describes the mercy of God as compassion that never fails which is renewed every morning that every sinners may not utterly be consumed.

- Exodus 34:6 reveals mercy as an act of forgiveness for numerous and all kinds of sin for as many as the sinners can be.

- Nehemiah 9:31 makes us to see God in His mercy as a gracious God towards sinners

- Psalm 40:11 reveals mercy of God as a loving-kindness

- Psalm 89:2 makes to understand that the mercy of God can be described as His faithfulness (Lam 3:23); He is forever faithful to every sinners who repent.

Many places in the Bible talks extensively about the mercy of God toward sinners; He call out for sinners to repent, He dialogues with them that he may forgive them, He awaits sinner for their salvation, He forgives and forget totally the sins of every man, and then He gave Himself for the redemption of every sinners.

And to His children who have one way or the other have transgressed, God has given us the great mediator, our great lawyer, intermediary and intercessor (1 John 2), that Satan our adversary will always be disgraced whenever we are ready to return unto God.

CHAPTER 4:
OBTAINING MERCY

Romans 9:15-16

"What shall we say then? Is there unrighteousness in God? God forbid. For He saith to Moses, I will have mercy on whom I will have mercy, I will have compassion on whom I will have compassion."

This scripture above makes us to understand that mercy don't just come anyhow, or is accidental, apart that God many times show compassion to His creation in generally as I have discussed above, but yet His mercy has being predestined and or preserved specifically for some people.

Nevertheless it is programmed for some people; those who deserves it by work, those who fervently asked for it, those who God has chosen or desire to use.

Obtaining mercy by work

- By our act of mercy

Matthew 5:7

"Blessed are the merciful: for they shall obtain mercy"

Jesus in His earthly life really gave us a clue about how to obtain mercy by work; He did this when He spoke about forgiving or having mercy on one another as emphasized in Matt 18:33. He made us to vividly understand that for one to obtain mercy he must be someone who is merciful; who is compassionate toward his fellow men. He taught us more when He added in a phrase in His "The Lord's prayer" that "forgive us our trespasses as we forgive those who trespass against us", then you will see that He later made further emphasis on that part alone that we may understand that we can obtain an easy forgiveness when we forgive. Not only on the forgiveness, but also goodness, faithfulness toward God and man, our compassion toward the poor and the less privilege, and also toward His people. That is why we cannot rule out love of one another in this matter, it will be easy for us to be merciful when we have love planted at the center of our heart. So if you are not merciful, if you think acquiring wealth by fraud or oppressing others is normal, then it's a waste of time asking for mercy; if you cannot forgive easily, then mercy is far from you and every form of gimmicks is a great enemy to the mercy of God.

- Our service unto God counts a lot

Nehemiah told God to reward him because of what he had done concerning Jerusalem especially the building of the wall. Many people pray for mercy, but sometimes it may be that God will expect something worth obtaining mercy from you before He would shower His compassion on you. Do you give to the poor, do you forgive easily, are you merciful, how well do you serve in God's vineyard, how well do you pay your tithe and offerings, how well do you sow seed, how well do you contribute to the progress of the work of God, and how well do you obey His word? Those who oppress will never be close to it even if they seek thoroughly for it. In the book of Isaiah 1:11-15, God was trying to tell the Israelites that He cannot be bribed by gifts or offering but rather He need a faithful work from them that will benefits the condition their environments or society. God want people to feel as He feels toward the creations and so also to seek after His precepts.

Jehoshaphat was a man that should die with Ahab. He was an absence-minded and a negligent person, which is very dangerous for a child of God to be. He must have known the kind of person Ahab was; he must have heard of his dealings with Elijah the prophet of God, he must have learnt about his errors and how he had contributed to the plans of his evil wife Jezebel, and then also

Jehoshaphat witnessed the drama that took place in Ahab's palace before he went to war against Ramoth-gilead when some prophets began to prophecy lies and he also saw what happened between those false prophets, Ahab and that one true prophet Micaiah the son of Imla (2 Chron 18). Yet he lost his mind by following Ahab to war, and then at war he played the fool when Ahab made an idiot out of him by giving him his robe to wear. All this is enough for him to perish with Ahab. But at the point when he supposed to die by his foolishness after the enemies thought he was the king whom they have purposely fought to kill, he cried and the Bible says God moved them to depart from him. On a normal day those enemies would have decided not to consent with his excuse seeing him in Ahab's robe, they would have thought one way or the other he must greatly have something to do with Ahab and still consider him as an enemy; is either he will be killed or held captive, but God decided to have mercy on him. Then in 2 Chronicles 19, God told him through Jehu the son of Hanani that if not for the fact that God saw something good in him he would have died following the enemy of God. Remember Ahaziah Jehoshaphat's grandson also did the same thing but he was killed just because unlike his grandfather there's nothing inside him that would have made him obtained mercy.

- A work done by our progenitors either from father or from mother

However, we can also obtain mercy as a result of what our ancestors has done, talking of our fathers, mothers, fore fathers, grandfathers and grandmothers. It may be a special kind of service that they may have engage themselves in which they were very much faithful to, that God through it will purpose in His heart to repay the children, it may be at the result of the covenant God had made with the ancestors as we have read concerning Abraham. God made the Israelites to understand that they should not think that their righteousness had made them to possess the Canaan land, after all it was called the promise land; that is, it was a covenant God made with their fore-fathers: father Abraham, Isaac and Jacob. God made them to understand that they were not qualified to possess the land but had obtained mercy through the covenant He made with Abraham Isaac and Jacob.

The case of Mephibosheth is also a good example. He was the son of Jonathan David's very good friend but he was also crippled. The Bible made us to understand that David was a man who hated the crippled and such handicapped people (2 Samuel 5:8), but because David knew the passion Jonathan had for him when he was alive he decided to repay his son Mephibosheth by having mercy upon him; he caused him to sit at his table

(2 Samuel 9). Mephibosheth obtained mercy only because his father had contributed to the plan and purpose of God for David's life.

A man who was an infamous armed robber was arrested by the local vigilante and was taken to their chief in the town who condemned him to die with his accomplice torturing them first by hitting 6 inches nails on their head. His fellow accomplice died at the result, but he alone was restored back to life. He said a man appeared in white went to him; held his hand and rescued him from the dump they were dumped at. Why did he obtain this mercy, when he shared more about his life we got to know that he was a descendant to Bishop Samuel Ajayi Crowther, the first African Anglican Bishop and the man who translated the King James Version Bible into Yoruba language; first African language the Bible was translated into in the 1800s. I was made to understand that God saw his progenitor's service unto Him and by that God rescued him.

Sometimes God have mercy upon the husband because of the wife and vice versa, sometimes God have mercy on the children because of the parents and vice versa.

- Obtaining mercy through the cry of our prayers for it

Sometimes it pleases God to willingly have mercy on someone but the pride of heart and self-guilt won't make us to ask for mercy.

Talking about self-guilt, when you preach to some people today even right on their sick bed ready to die, they'll tell you they have gone very far and they don't think they can obtain mercy. Satan the master manipulator wrought self-guilt in one's heart and makes him or her to think that forgiveness is impossible. But God said in Isaiah 1:18 that *"Come now, and let us reason together, saith the Lord: though your sins be as scarlet, they shall be as white as snow, though they be red like crimson, they shall be as wool"*. What God need is you coming to Him as you are and state your case, for He said return to me and I will return to you. He is so merciful to everyone who asks for it.

However, when we talk about pride I will like to remind us of the case of King Saul and King David, both as a king in Israel and they both committed sin. Saul sought for honour but David sought for mercy, and so Saul was rejected, but David was forgiven. David knew the efficacy of mercy so never joked with it; he sought for mercy till he died. David never thought about how heinous his sins might be, he always had it at the back of his mind that God is merciful and so he asked for that mercy and God gave him.

James 5:15-16

"And the prayer of faith shall save the sick, and the Lord shall raise him up, and if he had committed sin, they shall be forgiven. Confess your fault one to another, that ye may be healed. The effectual fervent prayer of the righteous man availeth much"

God doesn't at one time neglect the cry for mercy; from a sinner, from the poor, from the little ones and from the church of God.

- Intercession

Nevertheless when a man is being interceded for, God will love to be merciful. God told Ezekiel that if He would see only one man to stand in the gap between the sinful nation and Him, He would forgive. There are many people that have obtained mercy and they don't really know the reason why they have obtained it. In this case people are very much ignorant, when a prophecy comes out for the new year people tend to make a tight follow up to see if it will come to pass most especially the negative ones, and when it seems that it does not come to pass in that year, then people especially the unbelievers will think the prophecy is fake. But they won't know that as God chose people to be a watchman to give a warning by a prophecy so also He chose people to intercede that the negative prophecy may not come to pass. Some negative prophecy are actually to warn people that they might change their ways (like the case of the watchman according to Ezekiel 33) and that the children of God may intercede to avert or stop it in coming to pass. So a child of God who understands the nature of God will only give thanks to God who had withheld or averted the negative prophecy because he had acknowledged that mercy of God is involved.

That is why as a child of God one needs to cultivate the habits of interceding. I usually tell my brethren in my ministry then, whenever we are having a prayer session that our last prayer point should be an intercession, and therefore we will pick one person we know irrespective of how close or how far he or she may be to us, to pray for them individually. Thank God for "The Gap Filler Prayer Outreach Ministry International (GFPOM)" and other intercessory ministries around the world which God has been using to stand in the gap to the lost soul and to the captives, to the church of God, and to the nations around the world. Through intercession there are many aversions of any sort of atrocity and calamity, God has been saving souls and signs and wonders are happening and there are many testimonies. Intercession often provokes the efficacy of mercy.

Those who God has desired to use

Going back to Romans 9:14-15

"As it is written, Jacob have I loved, but Esau have hated. What shall we say then? Is there unrighteousness with God? God forbid. For He saith to Moses I will have mercy on whom I will have mercy on who I will have mercy, and I will have compassion on whom I will have compassion"

Some critical minds would have been curious about this statement in the Bible; many people may question why did God really had mercy on Jacob and not on Esau even before they were born. Many-a-times when God will use someone for a particular purpose in life, He will deal with that fellow with His mercy and compassion. What someone else will do and results in fatality or death, he or she will survive when engaged in it. There will be all-round favour, and there will be a divine help whenever he or she is choked. One way or the other when Satan perceives a call upon a life, he will want to do things as much as possible to terminate the destiny of such life and or try to divert such person away from the road of the glorious purpose. But along the process there will be a divine intervention. Even though we are made to understand that Jacob obtained mercy but yet he experienced hardship first. What I am saying in essence is that the basic purpose for the mercy Jacob had obtained was that God wanted to establish His covenant made with Abraham through Jacob and not Esau, and we all understand that by the virtue of that promise God had to change his name to Israel like He had changed Abraham's, and by the name Israel, is the nation being established and made known. Esau not obtaining mercy at the other hand as we thought doesn't mean he was a total cast away, as a matter of fact, he was established as a nation long before Jacob was, no hardship was recorded concerning him before he was established; neither did he go sojourning in another land, but the truth remains that he wasn't established by the covenant of God. So the mercy Jacob obtained was the possession of the covenant to be used as His own.

Pastor Adeboye of RCCG shared his testimony of how God has been protecting him since his childhood, and thereafter in his adulthood how God had singled him out from among his sinful friends to now become the General Overseer. The truth is anyone whom God have a special purpose for, despite the fact of any sort of disqualification or how faulty his past might be or how guilty he may be, he will surely receive mercy from God. God knew the end from the beginning and know who is worthy and fit for His assignment and so He preserves His own vessel with great care. There are many great men and women of God who God had rescued from condemnations which another person cannot escape. Mary Magdalene could have been stoned elsewhere but God who was in need of her for the support of Jesus ministry made her to obtained mercy. The mad man of Gadara was destined to be a great witness and evangelist for God and so he obtained mercy. Paul the apostle was a great persecutor of the Christians but out of his colleagues in the law school going around stoning the "enemies of the law" he was set apart.

He shared his testimony in 1 Tim. 1:12-16

"And I thank Christ Jesus our Lord, who hath enable me, for that he counted me faithful, putting me into the ministry; [13]who was before a blasphemer, and a persecutor, and injurious: but obtained mercy, because I did it ignorantly in unbelief.[14] And the grace of our Lord was exceedingly abundant with faith and love which is in Christ Jesus. [15]This is a faithful saying, and worthy of acceptation, that Christ Jesus came to the world to save sinners; of whom I am chief. [16]Howbeit for this cause I obtained mercy, that in me first Jesus Christ might show forth all longsuffering, for a pattern to them which should hereafter believe on him to life everlasting."

Here above is Paul talking in gratitude of how the mercy of God over his life had made him to be peculiar. Remember I said earlier that when grace grows to become exceeding then it appears to become mercy because at that stage it operates like mercy. And here in the above passage Paul was talking about the grace of Christ over him as being an exceeding and abundant, that is, he obtained mercy by been chosen for a special assignment for God who he had once despised through the love in Christ Jesus. Also in his recount about his past according to Acts 22, he was the only one, who heard the voice of Jesus Christ among his accomplice travelling together, and God made an arrangement for him, such a one that his accomplice will not be suspicious that where they are taking him is where he would be converted to a Christian. He was taken to Ananias, note what was said concerning him in that Acts 22:12 that *"….a devout man according to the law, having a good report of all the Jews which dwell there"*. Paul didn't say he was a Christian, that is to say those people who took him there never recognized him as a Christian, and so they could not think that Paul would be converted from there, if they had knew, something else may have happened which would have jeopardized his call.

Mercy doesn't come accidentally as I have said, it does not come on a platter of gold, when God said He would have mercy on who He will have mercy, it means He will not give out mercy to just anybody as He does with grace; His mercy has a purpose, He gives it to people who will value it and to people who will tell others how they have obtained it. He gives it to people who will yield fruits for Him and fulfill His purpose. Those who had obtained mercy are usually those who have had much experience to teach the people.

Sometimes when God will justify Himself about the privilege of His mercy over someone, He will cause that fellow to do something that will make Him obtain mercy, there will be a grace (like I said mercy and grace works together many times); an inner force and that will push someone to do something no other person can think of doing. For example: Can a man fight God? But Jacob was giving the grace to wrestle with Him, when God will bless Solomon He put it in his mind to sacrifice a thousand burnt offerings unto the Lord, Abraham passed the test for mercy when he gladly accepted those visitors and did a very good feast to entertain them, and by that wonderful hospitality he was justified. Then Joshua and Caleb, their lives made me to see clearly the statement of truth about the mercy of God as written in the above reference of Romans 9:16 that truly it is not of him that willeth nor of him that runneth, but of the Lord that showeth mercy. They both obtained mercy and was able to be qualified to enter the promise land: the land that so many people are not privileged to gain, and these people included the great Prophet and the first high Priest of the Old Testament which are Moses and his brother Aaron, do you remember Aholiab the son of Ahisamach and Bezaleel the son of Uri those whose wisdoms were impacted by God to build all the furniture and to weave all the curtains of which was perfectly accomplished by them to be used for sacred use in the tent where the glory of God descended on, the seventy elders which saw the glory of God at the tabernacle and which had also shared in the holy spirit inside Moses, even Medad and Eldad which the spirit rested on even though they were absent at the meeting, some of those sons of Aaron which were consecrated by Moses to minister as priest at the tent, and everyone else who had partook in the Manna (the meal of the angels), they all died in the wilderness, but saved everyone under the age of twenty as God had spoken and then Joshua and Caleb of which simply because they were moved to do what all other congregations could not do and which is the simple proclamation of their faith and strength in God Most-High. We could say Joshua had experienced much with Moses which could have made him to do what he did, but Caleb was nobody but one of the twelve spies sent to spy the Canaan land just like the other rebels or just another insignificant Israelite, but was made to obtain mercy.

And this situation can be likened to our Heavenly race; many will be expected to be qualified but only those who obtained mercy will be those who will inherit it. Then if that is the case, we will need to pray to God more for grace to do something that will make us to obtain mercy and that the Heavenly land might be our portion.

CHAPTER 5:
MERCY AS A RESIDUE

As we have discussed at the beginning of this book that mercy is simply not getting what we deserves, which is as a sinner not getting the judgement as we deserved it. And I said mercy can go beyond that, when grace (which is getting something one doesn't deserve) gets into a level of extraordinary or great or abundant, then mercy can be said to be involved.

Romans 9:16

"So, it's not of him that willeth nor of him that runneth, but of the Lord that showeth mercy"

When we are talking about mercy as a residue we are actually saying that when all strength are lost in one particular condition, or when our ignorance or negligence has brought us to a certain situation whereby danger is inevitable no matter how well we tried to avoid it, and such like that of which we are going to discuss more in this chapter, then in such tight situations if God's mercy is what is left, then we will surely escape the unfortunate eventuality.

Mercy as residue blocks the way of sin

In 1 Cor. 7:7-9 Paul made a brief statement on a special grace given to every man for the discipline and containment against any form of lust of flesh while discussing on the issue of marriage, he made it known that each person has that different kind of that sufficient grace (Paul called it "gift") as he said in the reference *"For I would all men were even as myself* (that is in the matter of self-control –the restraint of sexual desire in Paul).*But every man hath his proper gift of God, in one after this manner, and another after that* (that is some are discipline over food, some doesn't get angry easily, and so on)".Paul was simply saying every man has each of his own strong positive temperament to tackle works of flesh.

And however we all have weaknesses individually and that is what the devil preys on in our lives. The strategy of Satan is to trap us where we are weak, where we lack this sufficient grace as the Bible says in James 1:14 that *"Every man is tempted, when he is drawn away of his own lust, and entice"* and that is why we need to be very careful not to walk by the grave of our buried old man because that is when they got revived and grab us by the leg, and that was why I said earlier that grace often have limitations.

But the involvement of Mercy does not only deliver from judgement; it can also save one from committing errors when one lacks the strength to resist. I usually tell people that as a young believer I have had the chances of engaging in fornication not once, it's not that I have the power or gift to resist it like Paul as I have discussed above, but God in His infinite mercy, by one way or the other and beyond my capacity and reasoning will just rescue me. Sometimes we may find ourselves through our carelessness or negligence in a certain condition where we may not have the grace to contain it. What has happened to big men and women of God that has made them to compromise, will be the one another person not as highly spiritual as them will escape, not that they are much more closer to God but it is only because they obtained mercy. The truth is those that fell had no intention of falling but they can't just contain themselves at that moment. And sometimes those that have fallen fell because they never believed they would fall; they thought they have the grace against the day of temptation.

Sometimes when at the point where telling lies will be the only option for your escape, at the point whereby you almost roughly fight back a public offence which could have implicated and stain your identity as a believer, or when a kind of a frustration that could make one to commit an offence as a believer whether caused by our spouse or by our bosses or by our neighbors or by our co-workers happens and one think there is no choice but to react, and as you are thinking about trying to react so also the devil awaits to take advantage of you and as you take off the first step and so the Holy Spirit sounded within you and yet you disregard the solemn voice because you are already burning, then He uses something to divert the situation: to divert that moment you are about to commit adultery He may use anybody to give you a call and then your mind opens, or reverse or make something interfere that condition that asked for a lie to survive, or disturbed the network that moment you are tempted to watch pornography on the internet video, or just make any diversion away from the moment you are about committing any sin. Even sometimes when at that moment you are powerless to resist the temptation that could result to profaning God's name, then by mercy you receive a brand new grace to overcome and this is different from diverting the situation.

Mercy affects eternal destiny

There is a secret I will like to reveal here concerning the great efficacy of mercy, when a man seek thoroughly to be worthy for the kingdom of God at the end the most important thing for him to ask is mercy, for the Bible says not of him that willeth nor of him that runneth but of that showeth mercy. Many are truly called and many truly responded to the call, for the Bible didn't say in those many that are called, few responded, no, but furthermore says few were chosen. Now I give you this; many who are truly called will lose Heaven, it may sound disturbing but it is true but I pray we shall not be among them in Jesus name. A man can be known for his fervent devotion to the work of God for decades but eventually one way or the other have a bad eternal destiny, and at other hand a man could have every of his past years living in sins and at his last days to his demise may receive salvation and have a good eternity. If you will agree with me that our Great God knows the ending from the beginning, and then you should agree with me that He definitely know your eternal destiny which certainly you don't really know. Then if so, boasting the assurance of being a Heaven candidate as a result of your confidence in the thought of how holy you live your life should be little, but our race depends on the mercy of God so we need to be asking for it every day. Even apostle Paul also requested for the prayers from the church. It is in the nature of God to keep us from falling, to help us when we are weak.

It endures when confidence in prayer seems to fail

When mercy is involved in a case, it will not matter how powerless you are in a certain condition, you will achieve what a prayer warrior will not achieve.

When mercy is involved in a case, the how weak you are in fasting and prayers will not matter.

There is a story we were told about a man who is fervent in prayer, he mostly teaches about binding and loosing in the moment of prayer, and I'm quite sure he will be very familiar to demonology. But when it got to a time when his wife wanted to give birth, after she had laboured for so many hours, the man began to pray fervently; he binded everything needed to be binded and loosed everything needed to be loosed but it seems not working, then at a point he broke down into tears and simply said "Oh God, have mercy on me, have mercy on my wife" not long to that moment his wife gave birth.

David did not joke in the prayers for mercy because he knew the efficacy of it, even though he was a man of valour spiritually and physically yet sometimes he just admits that his enemies are more stronger than him (Psalm 142:6), and then he will just pray for mercy (Psalm 56; 57).

Christians should not underestimate the involvement of Satan in the battle of life, the more a Christian underestimate the battle of life, the more Satan takes advantage. Many Christians believed that when they are born-again, no more battle, take it or leave it Satan himself is always happy for such believes, so as he afflicts little by little so he will make you believe it is just some test of faith, and so you will disregard engaging in spiritual warfare until you are spiritually molested totally. And some believed that as long as they can pray all night like Jesus did they are able to conquer all, fine, but remember that Jesus was stressed out to extent of sweating blood when He was about to face the last battle at Gethsemane, but the Bible says that the angels came to Him and helped him; Jesus at the moment in Gethsemane wished God would just take away the suffering, closed to became a compromised mission, but the Bible says the angel came and help Him. Therefore as a man Jesus knew the suffering of human and so for that reason He intercedes always for us because He knows we cannot handle all our problems alone. Some stages in Christian life needs a Christian to quickly cry out for mercy to overcome. And many times it is mercy of God that shows the area where we can concentrates our prayers on.

When ability fails, Mercy makes way where there seems to be no way

In the case of mercy, the race will not be for the swift as we have read in the reference above. When the Bible says the food is not for the wise, this does happen also in the case of mercy. There are many books, seminars, talk shows and so on, that speaks on how to get riches, giving some ideas, motivational speeches and so on. All this won't matter for you to succeed if mercy is involved. Many times all what we have read about or what we have tried by the skills received at seminars or what we have put into practice what we have heard from motivational talk show usually seems not working, or the enemies may prey on your intellect and hard work, and all this always cause loss of hopes and frustrations and the future seems so unsure because already you have been diverted from your dream career, and you think what else can I do. There is only one thing you can do to be back on track and succeed; cry unto God for mercy, in His mercy He will intervene and breakthrough your situation. Nothing else works more perfectly as that of the involvement of the mercy of God to succeed again.

Psalm 136:12-14;

"[12]With a strong hand, and with a stretch out hand…

[13]To Him who divided the red sea into parts…

[14]And made Israel to pass in the midst of it: for His mercy endureth forever"

The Bible is saying here that the journey of Israel was at the result of the mercy God took on them. That is, the sea could have been a great hindrance for them, but God cleared it away. Therefore this passage applies to every Christian that relying on the mercy of God makes way where there seems to be no way. When we read that Psalm 136 very well, we will see that every success of Israel through their journey is backed up with the mercy of God, which means that every Christian should rely on the mercy of God for breakthrough in their journey in life and not in their powers, remember it's not of him that runneth neither of him that willeth, but of the Lord that shows mercy.

When barrier is so great before you; ask for mercy, when you are frustrated; ask for mercy, when strength and gift fails, then ask for mercy.

Mercy saves from snares and sudden danger

Brethren it is a lie if we say that Children of God cannot be a victim of the atrocities going on in the world today, as a matter of fact the Christians are the most targeted victims. Satan want to make sure that everything works together against Christians, so he always tries to ensnare us spiritually and physically. But sometimes we almost fall victim and sometimes we actually fall victim; by our ignorance, by self-confidence or over-zealousness which usually be a product of Self-righteousness, it may be through negligence, and disobedience, these are usually what makes a Christian a snare victim or endangered victim this days, and because most times we underestimate the devil. However, the mercy of God is so wonderful that even though you find yourself to be a victim of snare or danger, yet when you call upon God for His mercy it will bring salvation. As we have earlier revealed from the story of Jehoshaphat, even though he deserved to die because he went to war along-side with the enemy of God, but yet by the mercy of God he was delivered.

Mercy of God saves beyond human comprehension, and that is why you see people escape fatal event without a comprehensive explanation. Long time ago there was a particular riot along the route I usually take when going to church. On a normal day it used to be a kind of a motor park for commuters and where hawkers sell their goods, but on that very day I notice that the atmosphere was different; everywhere was quiet as if there was a curfew, no hawker was there even right in the afternoon, but as an innocent young boy, even though I was surprised at the atmosphere but I kept walking peacefully, as I reached the church on that day someone approached me and asked of my brother and I replied that he is coming, but not quite long my brother also appeared as everything seems normal, but we were not really told what happened and likewise we also didn't bother to ask, so we entered the church, and at the closing time again but this time my brother and I were together walking home and this time it was 8 pm at night, and when we pass by the same route we took when going to church, we both noticed that it was again as calm as when we were going ealier in the afternoon and again which was very unusual but we kept walking peacefully as we discussed about what may have caused it. But when we got home on that day, then we were fully told about what had really happened at the place; we were told that a serious riot took place twice at the juncture, but our research showed that it happened few minutes before we reached and pass the area, and began thereafter again few minutes after we have passed when we were going to church in the afternoon, and when we were returning to our house in the evening it happened same way it had happened when we were going in the afternoon, what had caused it to stop for us to pass I wouldn't know, but the riot event was made to stop by the intervention of God. That is what mercy does; it rescues from danger. An adage says when it remains few steps for the son of a righteous to fall inside a ditch, lightning will work as light to illuminate his path. The intervention of the mercy of God is so great beyond man's comprehension. It is responsible for those many narrow escapes and mysterious escapes that are unexplainable; escapes from terrorist attack, from kidnappers, from accidents of any kind, natural hazards, and so on.

Mercy makes pardon

There are many people that of a truth it seems that they deserve to die, there are nations that have forgotten God and likewise there are nations that are really blind to the right and perfect perception of God, of which they have mistaken their idol as the Almighty God. Of a truth they are worth to be totally wiped out has God had decreed concerning the Amalekites, because they have despise the true God and harbor hatred towards His people. Yet God still look down with mercy; He gives rain to both good and the bad and gives a simple principle to guild the whole humanity and to live upon even though it doesn't guarantees the great salvation; and which is "whatever a man soweth he shall reap", but His ultimate desire is that everyone should be saved, and that is why Jesus Christ is being presented to us as our Lord, that whosoever believes in Him should not perish but have everlasting life and that is a great compassion from our great God.

The mercy of God in the ministry of man makes him have the fullness of testimony, when a person who fast and pray, or struggles to live a fulfilled life is still crawling, a man who has received mercy will be glorified even with the little thing he does.

CHAPTER 6:
BEHOLD I WILL DO A NEW THING

This is the very part I love most about the great Mercy of God most high; that is, when it creates a new Beginning. We have discussed in the previous chapter of how mercy intervenes in some situations and we have made it known that whenever a man reached a point when he is stucked and cannot move any much further neither can he turn back then when mercy rise up to intervene and thereafter will be a breakthrough. And thus mercy creates a new thing; a new beginning

A New Thing

When we talk about the word "A New Thing" then definitely there will be an old thing; a thing in existence before which must have a blemish, a limitation, a fault, worn out, old, inactive, outdated, and so on.

A new thing happens in three ways:

A New Thing as an Upgrade (renewal, replacement)

This is when the initial material is old or outdated and ready to be inactive. When a condition is no more fits for the situation on ground. In Genesis 18, when God visited Abraham and told him that they will be visited according to the time of life and they will have a son, Sarah laughed, she thought her situation at that time was outdated to be fit in for the condition; verse 11 says " *Now Abraham and Sarah his wife was old and well stricken in age; and it cease to be with Sarah after the manner of women*" that is, Sarah was very old that she had gone beyond child bearing, but when the mercy of God visited their family their story changed; Sarah's womb was 'updated', it was renewed, and that is the work of mercy. Have you been told that you also cannot bear the fruit of the womb again, or have you been told that your eyes cannot receive sight, or is there any part in your body that is inactive? Behold the Lord says He is going to have mercy on you by doing something new on that affected area and it shall be renewed, and so shall it be in Jesus name.

Hebrews 8 vs7-13;

"⁷For if that first covenant had been faultless, then should no place have been sought for the second. ⁸For finding fault with

them, he saith, Behold, the Lord, when I will make a new covenant with the house of Israel and with the house of Judah: [9]not according to the covenant I made with their fathers when I took them by the hand to lead them out of the land of Egypt; because they continued not in my covenant, and I regarded them not, saith the Lord. [10]For this is the covenant that I will make with house of Israel after those days, saith the Lord; I will put my laws into their mind, and write them in their hearts: and I will their God, and they shall be my people: [11]and they shall not teach every man his neighbour, and every man his brother saying, know the Lord: for all shall know me, from the least to greatest. [12]For I will be merciful to their unrighteousness, and their iniquities will I remember no more. [13]In that he saith, a new covenant, he hath made the first old. Now that which decayeth and waxeth old is ready to vanish away"

The above passage explained the outdated testament of which was used by Israel when they departed from Egypt. The testament involves laws including observing the days, sacrifices, moral constitution, and its penalties which included executions that is stoning etc. (but never be in any form of beheading), and all which are carried out by physical applications. The purpose of God for the covenant is to draw them unto Himself and to set them apart from other nations for a special fulfillment which is the coming and manifestation of the Lord Jesus Christ. The fault of the Old Testament was actually at the result of the lack of grace to fulfill its law by the Israelites. They found it difficult in obeying the Old Testament law, and so the more they disobey, the more they are punished and thus the law did made them enemies of God instead of drawing them closer. But the desire of God is actually made known in Deuteronomy 5:29 which says *"O that there were such an heart in them, that they would fear me, and keep all my commandment always, that it might be well with them, and their children forever"*. But by the mercy of God, instead of wiping them out totally because of their disobedience He rather replaced the covenant and by the renewal of the covenant a great grace was opened to every one through the death of Jesus Christ. The former covenant was limited to the Hebrews but the new one is now for the salvation of the whole world; to draw her closer to Him. We are given everything needed to serve God free and full of grace only by the enduring Mercy of God because this New covenant involves the death of Christ which replace animal sacrifices for the atonement of sins and of which it is done only once, the grace to become a child of God, the impartation of the new heart of worship as God promised in the book of Ezekiel 36;26 and 27, easy forgiveness, the grace to boldly go before God to ask for anything, the grace to worship God not through the means of anyone but through Christ only, and the eternal glory which awaits us that we might see these world and it's pleasure as vanity because what will be also upgraded is the heaven and the earth (Rev 21)

So who had told you that your sins cannot be forgiven or who told your consecration is costly, who told you it is too late to turn back and who told you that you have reached the point of no return. The mercy of God renews grace for you to get another opportunity that you might be worthy to be called the son or daughter of God and give you the grace to abide in Him.

And for everyone who is just receiving Christ as the Lord and personal savior, to them the Bible says there is no more condemnation to them and that those old things has passed away and everything has become New for the life is been renewed.

A New Beginning Out of an End (a modification)

A new beginning out of an end is, when the world thinks it has ended for you, then that is when the mercy of God brings about a new beginning of a new progress to happen. For an example when Joseph shared his dreams to his brothers, they sought to trash his destiny; they threw him inside the pit and thereafter he was sold into the foreign land. That could have been a 'full stop' to his dreams, but God intervene and convert his journey of slavery into a new journey for greatness. Unlike the first one discussed above, this is not a replacement or renewal of the old but rather new beginning out of the defected and deserted case modifying it to become an advantage. This is when God add a new chapter to 'the end' of the book of one's life; this is when a condition put a 'full stop' to the sentence of your life and God put a 'comma' underneath to become a 'semicolon' and thus the sentence continues; when the end matter becomes a starting point for a new beginning.

Job 14:7

"For there is hope of a tree, if it be cut down, that it will be sprout again, and that the tender branch thereof will not cease..."

When one is not dead there is still hope no matter the casualty, when life offers you a hopeless situation then the mercy of God will convert it to be a journey of a new destiny irrespective of the defects or blemish: maybe the amputation of the hand or leg, loss of eye sight or hearings and so on, as a result of casualties. Many people's destiny may have been averted because of such casualties. It will not be that God will perform a miracle and restore the loss at the cause of the casualty, but rather make a providence to begin a new life from that juncture; setting a new sail for a new journey of destiny either new destiny or the initial destiny.

We may be in the similar condition one way or the way, either by our negligence or disobedience or maybe the work of the enemies and have gotten us to a close, either by defection or desertion, the good news is God by His mercy can reverse the irreversible; He can still bring perfection out of defects, and bring greatness out of a deserted state, and thus make out of us an icon of hope to the others. He is [a merciful] God of all flesh, so is there anything too hard for Him?

A New Thing as a New Thing (a miracle)

Isaiah 43 vs 19

"Behold I will do a new thing; now it shall spring forth…"

When God made way through the sea, it was something that has never occurred before and by this action God was able to prove Himself as the Omnipotent God and to fight for His children. God knew there was a way already that could lead the Israelites away from the

Egypt before taking them through the route to the Red sea, God would have made the Egyptians to suffer in another way, but God chose to make them suffer in a way that has never come to mind of man.

When God says "Now it shall spring forth" it means that it is coming out from nothing, that is, it is not a conversion of defects neither a replacement of the old, (as discussed above). He won't even wait for the first condition to be irrelevant before He starts doing a new thing, but a new thing with its own beginning and with a brand new purpose and this often comes as a Miracle.

1 Corinthians 2:9

"But as it is written, Eye hath not seen, nor ear heard, neither have entered into the heat of man, the things which God has prepared for them that love Him"

He is still interested in doing wonders; something a man as never seen before, something that has never occurred to man before. He has made a virgin to give birth, He has once commanded a money out of the mouth of a fish, He multiplied five loaves of bread and two fishes to feed five thousand people, He walked on the sea. He is still interested in making dry bones to become a flesh, He can still turn water into wine and make oil out from an empty barrel. And of course He is still in great interest to use His children to demonstrate His power to do a new and wonderful thing: He used Peter and His shadows worked miracles, Paul's handkerchief became a supernatural healing material. Apostle (Dr) T.O Obadare of World Soul Winning Evangelical Ministry (WOSEM) said before he died that "Thank God that the word of Christ in John 14:12 was fulfilled in my life because Jesus raised a four day old corpse of Lazarus from the dead, but God did through me raised a forty day old corpse from the dead".

The truth is, God can still do miracles more than old times and still use us more than those He had used in time past, but there are limitations because many people these days just want to be receiving from God but don't really want God, and most vessels He want to use are not within the perimeter of His presence. But get it well that what the eyes hath not seen neither the ear hath heard are only prepared for those who LOVE Him and Him alone.

However, when a man obtains mercy, the miracle of a 'New Thing' will take place in his life, either giving him a new beginning or renewing the olds and outdated conditions of his life or just work a miracle in his life. Remember according to the reference in that Psalm 136 every great and wonderful things experienced by the Israelite were wrought only by the mercy of God.

CHAPTER 7:
A GREAT NEED FOR MERCY

Mercy is in God's nature and He is ready to make it known to all men; either to those who really know Him and those who are ready to know Him. By His mercy He made His name available for salvation unto everyone, I have come to realized that even though uttering "The Name Of Jesus" works perfectly for God's children yet God still honours it in the mouth of the backsliders and unbelievers when they obviously see that there is no way out of their siege and there's no other person they could go for help at their worst state other than God, and when they call upon Him He answers simply because He has decided to have mercy.

So are you still wallowing in wretchedness because of your sinful life and thought of escaping, embrace now the offer of His grace of salvation by asking for His mercy, come back to Him as He is humbly and tenderly calling, and He shall turn again onto you what you have lost (Jeremiah 29:11-14). I see the mercy of God as what can be sought for above anything else because it profits more than anything whatsoever one may be seeking for because it profits one till eternity.

There is a great need of mercy especially in this generation:

Over Our Individual Lives: That we may not succumb to the temptation that it is offering us: money, technologies, new knowledge, unrighteous wisdom, and upgraded plans of the darkness; and then its trouble, atrocities, untrustworthy relatives and so on which could be enough for us to compromise. And even when it seems we have wandered away from the presence of the Almighty God and have found ourselves unfit to be back where God had wanted us to be initially, the mercy of God will intervene in our infirmities and make resolution that we might be back up on our feet again.

In The Families: Many marriages need repair by the intervention of the Almighty Father in Heaven because they're established on a wrong foundation. When a family crumbles it affect the church and then affects the nation. There are many wrong choices of partner and people tend to choose more in a wrong way, because most men has let their erections give them directions, and most ladies have allowed peer pressure and self-indulgence to control their entire life, and thus sexual immoralities and an unwanted pregnancy became the other of the day, and then it leads to a wrong marriage. Wrong marriage produces wrong breeding and wrong breed results to the children of Belial and children of Belial creates a bad society and bad societies constitutes nuisance which thus affects the nation.

But the good news is, God's mercy can remold the family and making the wrong couples to become right for themselves irrespective of how faulty the foundation might be; one way or the other He can renew a family, and divorce which is the great enemy of marriage will be stopped when mercy is involved because it will stop the siege against the marriage.

In The Church Of God: There is much entanglement of the church to the world today, I tell you there is no generation of the church that is worse than every new generation because every new generations unleashes new ideas, new wisdom (or doctrines) and new conspiracies from the evil world. But church today seems to think there is no great need for mercy; they thought been a born again Christian as ruled out the battle of life. But the truth there is that when you are on the Lord's side, you have chosen the right side, but choosing the right side doesn't mean you will not fight because the wrong side is always there to antagonize everything on the right side.

However now, there is a need to pray to God for mercy over the church against the evil wind; of rebellion, hypocrisy, lovelessness, pride, prayerlessness, filthiness and disunity. The truth is Satan have received a great success in two things against the church; the love of money and disunity, but it seems that the disunity is what has now become the other of the day what I called "The Paul-Apollo Syndrome", we tend to always look for the unfit and the incompetent "prosperity preacher's" church and with those "subverted" doctrine and we tend to be on each other's tail instead of interceding more, tell your truth as given by God and stop pointing fingers, of which is our main business. And as a matter of truth I have sought to know the perfect church, and searched through their doctrine but I have come to discover that no church really is perfect but just trying to be perfect, and that is why the church needs deliverance through the mercy of God. The song writer wrote: "

Dear dying Lamb, Thy precious blood

Shall never lose its power,

Till all the ransomed ones of God

Be saved, to sin no more:

Be saved, to sin no more,

Be saved, to sin no more;

Till all the ransomed ones of God,

Be saved to sin no more". When church stands together the nation will have her spiritual strong hold solidified more.

The Nation: When the Babylonians invaded Israel, their beautiful temple of Solomon; the pride of Israel, was demolished and then lost its pride. What is the pride of the Church if her nation is siege? The nation needs to be interceded for, especially in this generation; where her people engages in corruption, bloodshed, secret conspiracies against her people, persecution of the saints and the Church, Occultism, kidnapping and human sacrifice and thus defiling the land, and the blood of those that are shed kept crying for vengeance upon the nation and those that are innocent are affected. Brethren there is a great need for mercy, standing as individual, and together as a family and as the church of God we can achieve a great global deliverance for the nations of the world, that the Lord Himself will be happy to return sooner to rapture the great number of the faithful ones. The question is only "will He find faith?" and this is not an absolute negative statement toward the faith, and that is why we should strive to give positive answers to that "O yes our Lord, here is our still-standing good faith by your grace".

In Summary

The mercy of God is needed as solution to all strange and emergency problem: when you are in serious problem, cry for mercy; when you are at the middle of tumult, cry for mercy; when you are kidnapped, cry for mercy; when you are in a long time child labour, cry for mercy; when you get evil report, cry for mercy; when you are at the edge of failure, cry for mercy; when it seems you are not getting good results of your hard work, cry for mercy; when you are under siege, cry for mercy; when you are in great doubt, ask for mercy; if you are depressed, cry for mercy; need salvation and deliverance? Ask for mercy; you think you have backslidden? Cry for mercy. As a minister of God, you are in need of great manifestation over your congregation, cry for mercy; are you in need of great miracle, cry for mercy; and for every great needs mercy is greatly needed, and for a great mercy God is greatly needed.

PRAYERS

Confession:

Exodus 34:6-7

"⁶And the LORD passed by before him (Moses), and proclaimed, The LORD, The LORD God, merciful and gracious, longsuffering, and abundant in goodness and truth, ⁷keeping mercy for thousands, forgiving iniquity and transgression and sin, and that will by no means clear the guilty; visiting the iniquity of the fathers upon the children's children, unto the third and to the fourth generation."

Lamentation 3:21

"²¹This I recall to my mind, therefore have I hope. ²²It is of the Lord's mercies that we are not consume, because His compassion fail not. ²³they are new every morning: great is thy faithfulness."

Oh LORD we praise you for your merciful and gracious nature, and we proclaim again that oh LORD you are glorious, merciful, awesome, and gracious in your ways. We thank You for the forgiveness of our sins irrespective of the degree and gravity. We thank You for your great patient and longsuffering by which you have spared the lives of so many sinners even in their stagnant ignorant states.

Oh LORD we beg to be merciful over every trespasses individual and collective; of the church and of the nation; our negligence, our pride, our selfish ambition, our unbelief and all our unrighteousness.

Oh LORD we pray as Moses did to please help us to see Your face once more in our generation, we pray that you touch our individual lives that our lives may never be the same again.

Oh LORD we pray that by Your mercy You will reveal yourself to the lost souls, revive the backsliders, and rescue the perishing.

Let Your mercy be showered upon the hopeless, the poor, those in captivity whatsoever and let them feel Your goodness and compassion.

Let every dry bone receive life, turn every miserable ending into beautiful beginning, and make way miraculously where there seems to be no way.

Oh Lord, by your mercy visit our foundations; of our nations, of our churches, of our families and of our individual lives.

We pray for every nation still under the bondage of Satan, that they will receive the divine encounter, and that every bondage may be loosed that they may turn unto the Lord Jesus for salvation. And every killing and wars, every corruptions and unfaithfulness should be visited by God's mercy.

We pray for every people of God working earnestly for the kingdom of God either on the mission field or at the sanctuary that their needs might be met and sufficient more than enough.

Let thy mercy speak against every rising judgement and petition of the enemy against; individual lives of every believer, against the family, against the church of God and against the nation.

Let thy kingdom come Oh Lord, and let thy will be done.

Be thou glorified Oh Lord forever. In Jesus' precious name, Amen

www.ingramcontent.com/pod-product-compliance
Lightning Source LLC
Chambersburg PA
CBHW051654060726

47593CB00021B/1077